The Day in Punto Muerto

A Short Story by Wyatt Johnson

Inspired by *Big Iron*, A Song by Marty Robbins

The Territorial Marshall

The Territorial Marshall stood outside of a sheriff's office in an unremarkable boomtown. He reached into the saddlebag of his white-coated steed to find a pack of cigarettes as the morning sun beat down on them. The lawman shuffled through the disorganized bag before coming across the pack, nestled up against the piece of paper. He opened it in the saddlebag and pulled out a cigarette before striking a match on his boot and lighting it. The Marshall shook the match out and discarded it before taking a drag off of the smoke. He glanced down at his bag again, looking to close it up, but saw the paper once more. He pulled it out and muttered to himself as he read.

"John Falcon… El Paso Bank Robbery… Last seen in Arizona… One hundred dollar bounty… I'll find this bastard." He folded the paper and put it back in the bag before grabbing another, more worn piece of paper and unfolded it, revealing it to be a map. The Marshall was of Arizona, and hunting for the forlorn outlaw. "Let's find the nearest town. We'll start there." The grizzled and short, but very handsome, mustached Marshall mumbled.

Just then, the door of the sheriff's office swung open and the sheriff himself came down the steps. A sort of wild hair, as he was a man of few words, the Marshall thought to ask the sheriff if he knew anything about this outlaw, John Falcon. "Howdy Sheriff!" He called.

The Sheriff heard the call and approached the Marshall. "How can I help, Marshall?" The Sheriff got closer before continuing. He pointed at the badge on the Marshall's dark blue duster coat. "Couldn't help but notice the badge. It's nice to meet one of y'all Marshalls."

The Marshall showed the bounty paper of the outlaw to the sheriff. "You know of this feller? Says he was last seen here in Arizona." The sheriff appears surprised.

"John Falcon. Yeah, I hear he's found a home up in Punto Muerto. Just north of here." The Sheriff explained.

"Uh-huh… if you knew where he's been, why haven't you gone and got him?" The Marshall questioned. "Oh, don't let his age fool you," The Sheriff began.

"He's vicious and a killer. He done killed a rancher and his wife over a safe… He's… evil. Not to mention that robbery over in Texas. He killed too many good lawmen there…"

"I see…" The Marshall said. The sheriff patted him on the shoulder before walking off.

"Well, I'm off to get my whistle wet, Marshall. Good luck with that, if you decide to hunt him down. I'm sure only a Territorial Marshall could be the one to put that dog down." The Sheriff nodded as he walked away.

The Marshall looked back down at the map and tapped on the location with his gloved finger as he found it. "Punto Muerto. Well, that isn't very far." About a day's ride away, maybe a little more. The

Marshall looked at his horse that he had hitched to a post. "Maybe we could get a head start if we go right now, hey girl?" He said to the steed. The horse, who he talked to often, paid him no mind, just grazing. The Marshall chuckled as he unhitched the horse and climbed up on her. He adjusted his satchel before riding off into the desert to the town of Punto Muerto.

The Territorial Marshall rode for hours through the dry of the desert, hoping to get to Punto Muerto by the end of the day. He thought about what the sheriff said, about how he made John Falcon out to be a vicious, bloodlusting outlaw. The Marshall had heard all of this before. Many outlaws are described as if they are legends, and the Marshall always figured it was because of their body count. "Death is no small thing" His brother used to say, so he figured that the more someone had killed, the more fabled they had become. These outlaws weren't some messengers of the devil, but some trigger-happy dullards that get lucky sometimes, and that's how it's always been so far.

Thinking of that saying placed the Marshall's mind upon his brother. Like himself, his brother was a dealer of justice, although he was no Marshall or Ranger. He was free-spirited and rebellious, so he was more of a freelance bounty hunter.

The Marshall patted his steed as they travelled, encouraging her. She was his best friend. She's been with him through all of his hardships, through all of the bounties. He spoke to her with confidence that she would never share any secrets. The Marshall recalled the time when his wife had passed after the birth of his second child. When he went outside to recuperate and get away from the chaos that ensued, his horse was there for him to hug and wipe away his tears on.

It was around three in the afternoon when the Marshall stopped by a pond to get himself and his horse a drink. He looked into the settled and calm water of the pond before dipping his hand in to get a sip, and he saw the reflection of a mustached man who wore a black neckerchief around his neck. The Marshall looked at himself for a moment before taking a drink out of the water. His horse followed and drank what seemed like gallons on gallons of water.

"You thirsty girl? I'm sorry." The Marshall apologized to his steed after a small chortle. He approached her and reached into the saddlebag again, pulling out the entire pack of cigarettes. He slipped a cigarette into his mouth and put the rest of the pack in his satchel that laid upon his left hip.

The Marshall sat down after lighting his cigarette and threw his match into the pond. He looked over to his horse, who was still drinking. "Damn." he muttered, smiling. He puffed on his cigarette and it reminded him of his home in Tucson. He had two children he left with his brother-in-law while he was away. Said children always complained that he smoked, saying that they didn't ever like the smell. They were annoying that way, but the Marshall missed them anyway. He puffed on his cigarette and began to hum a tune that the cool water had reminded him of, and soon enough, the Marshall sang very quietly.

"All day I faced, the barren waste, without the taste of water… cool water…" He sang. The pair sat at the pond for a further half hour before riding off again.

As the sun began to set behind the hills, The Marshall realized that his goal of reaching the town before the end of the day was a pipe dream. He kept riding but also looked into the desert for places to camp. He settled on a patch of somewhat level land with a dry, old tree to hitch his steed to. There was even a log to sit on. He gathered stones and bits of drywood to make a fire with and As the shadows grew upon the desert thanks to the sun's departure, the Marshall noticed the lights of Punto Muerto in the distance, a good twenty mile ride. "Eh, we'll get there tomorrow. Bright and early." He said, hitching his horse to the tree and grabbing the bedroll off of the saddle.

After an hour, the Territorial Marshall sat at his makeshift campsite, staring into the flames of the fire he had made. An ember had popped out of the fire and landed upon his canvas satchel, which was quick to snap the Marshall out of his daydream. He slapped it out with his glove that laid on his leg as he sat on a log. He slapped the glove against his leg a few times to 'dust it off' and he glanced back over at his satchel that laid up against the log.

He grabbed a cigarette out of the pack in the satchel and lit it up, throwing the match into the fire. He puffed for a while and looked over at his horse, who grazed on the bits of grass that grew near the tree she was hitched to. He smiled at her before yawning. He took off his hat and duster and laid down on his bedroll. He threw his cigarette into the fire and unholstered his large six-shooter, laying it beside him and leaning its long barrel on the log. "Let's get some sleep!" He called to his best friend, and the Territorial Marshall closed his eyes.

He had a dream. The Marshall sat at his home in Tucson, in front of the brick fireplace in the parlour. He sat next to his brother, who, outside of this dream, had been killed in a duel with an outlaw. He also sat beside his children, but he was far more shocked that his brother was present. He looked to his brother who sat on his pockets up close to the fire like he did when they were younger, as they lived in the cold north of Utah in their youth. He scanned his brother up and down before the sibling turned his head to his brother, revealing the unseen side of it to be rotted and somewhat skeletal.

"Satan's hanging me tonight, brother. You'll be there to watch soon enough." The Brother said in a distorted and raspy voice. The Marshall slid back suddenly, startled by the voice and appearance of his late brother.

"What?" Was the only word the Marshall could muster up in response. Suddenly, the fire exploded in a fiery ball with the heat of a thousand suns. The house around them began to burn as the brother let out an unearthly laugh and the Marshall looked around fearfully and saw that his children were burning. He heard them scream, and he covered his ears. But then he looked up to see a support beam giving way as it burned. He threw his hand up to guard his face as the beam fell and just as it collided with the Marshall, he woke up.

Sweat ran down his face and he looked around the area. He saw the sun as it peered just over the hill, uncovering the shadowed grounds that night left behind. He looked at his horse and it looked back at him. It too appeared startled and if it had a mouth that could speak, it likely would have asked the Marshall if he had seen a ghost. He wiped the sweat from his face and stood up without saying a word and rolled up his bedroll after grabbing his iron and holstering it again.

The Marshall placed the bedroll on the steed's saddle and returned to the campsite to pick up his satchel and kick the dust into the campfire. He threw his satchel around his neck after taking the badge off his duster and rolling it up, placing it next to the bedroll. The Marshall clipped the badge to his vest and proceeded to unhitch his horse and ride off towards the town of Punto Muerto.

As he arrived to town from the south side, the Marshall peered around it and it seemed to be bustling even in the early morning. He heard the chattering of townsfolk, the whinnying of workhorses and a rumbling sound that appeared to be coming from his stomach. The lawman looked around the town square for a place to eat, and his eyes landed on a cafe that sat on the corner of the square. He approached it and hitched his steed to the hitching post which was decorated with a trough for drinking. The Marshall went up the stairs and entered the establishment through the swinging cafe doors.

Everyone inside that was enjoying a meal stopped suddenly and looked at the Territorial Marshall that had just entered the building. A brief silence befell the place for a moment as patrons scanned the stranger before the chattering resumed. He approached the counter and the tender did the same. "You want breakfast?" The tender asked. "Yes actually. What do you have?" The Marshall tapped the counter as the tender pulled out a menu from under it.

The lawman examined it for a moment, carefully looking through all of the options and soon enough and to his shock, his eyes fell on his favorite food of all time. "You can make chicken-fried steak?" He asked.

"Sure. We had a fella come in a while back that taught us how. I'll get it whipped up for you." The tender explained before disappearing into a back room behind the shelves full of drinks. The Marshall pulled up a seat and sat at the bar before lighting up another cigarette, preparing for a wait. He unintentionally eavesdropped on the conversation a seemingly well-off couple had behind him as they dined.

"That fella there that just came in, he's got the look of a bandit!" The woman observed. The man discreetly pointed to the Marshall, "Him? Didn't you see his badge? That's a lawman, and I bet he's here to do some business with that there pistol on his hip." The lack of a blue duster coat had revealed his firearm.

After a moment of waiting, the tender came out with a plate adorned with the food the lawman ordered. He placed it on the bar and the Marshall paid the cost of it. The tender returned to wiping down the counter and cleaning glasses as the lawman stared down at his meal, which to anyone without context, would appear as though he stared at a pile of pure gold. He inspected the chicken-fried steak, observing its crisp, brown skin which is lathered in the white and peppered country gravy. His stomach grumbled once more before he dug into the meal.

After a half hour, the Marshall left the establishment, wiping his lips with a handkerchief found in his back pocket. He looked around the town square and saw the Sheriff's office at the end of the street. He figured in his mind that that would be the best place to start looking for this outlaw. If the outlaw lived as a citizen in Punto Muerto, surely the Sheriff would know about it. The Marshall proceeded off the porch of the cafe and unhitched his horse before leading it across the way to the Sheriff's office.

The horse whinnied in remonstrance as she was led away from her source of water. The lawman looked around the square as it slowly grew busier. The gallows at the center of the square were rather grimly put AND built. Wagons hauling everything from hay to milk drive past and people make their commute around the town. At the base of the Sheriff's office, the Marshall once again hitched his steed to another hitching post which also had a trough, to the horse's delight.

"Be good, girl." The Marshall ordered as he walked up the steps. He reached his hand up to open the door, but it suddenly swung open into the building and a man was stepping out. Still looking into the building, he bumped into the Marshall catching him off guard.

"Oh, my apologies." The man said, placing his hand on his own chest. "It's no trouble." The Marshall assured. The man walked off and the lawman entered the office. He looked around briefly at the empty cells and his eyes fell on the sheriff who sat at his desk, pouring a glass of whiskey. Just then, the sheriff looked up and locked eyes with the Marshall just before glancing down at his badge. He squinted his eyes to read it.

"Well I'll be damned. If I knew a Territorial Marshall was gonna be coming into my office today, I'd have brought another glass from home." The Sheriff confessed, to which the Marshall laughed. "It's no problem Sheriff," He began as he sat down in front of the desk. "I just hope you can help me with a bit of an issue we've got."

"Oh?" The Sheriff stammered. "We have a problem?" To this the Marshall nodded.

"I've come to your town, Sheriff, because it's rumored there's an outlaw living here. So I'm here to take that outlaw back alive… or maybe dead. Depends." He specified.

"I can understand that, my friend." The Sheriff said before taking a sip of his whiskey. "I know of no outlaws here, just the scum on the roads from here to Santa Fe. What's the name of this outlaw?"

"John Falcon." The Marshall answered, and the Sheriff's face went cold. The Marshall noticed and asked, "Are you okay Sheriff? Do you know him?"

"He just left as you came in…" The Sheriff said, his expression changing to confusion. Suddenly, the Marshall stood up and ran to the door, swiftly opening it and stepping outside to the patio. He looked into the town square, but it was too late. The amount of commuters had doubled in the last minute, and John Falcon the outlaw was lost in the crowd. The Marshall returned to the Sheriff's desk and threw his hands on it.

"So you didn't know he was an outlaw?!" He questioned the Sheriff with fire in his words. "How was I supposed to know? It's not like he ever said!" The Sheriff attempted to retort.

"Of course he wouldn't have said!" The Marshall rubbed his face in irritation. The Sheriff sipped once more out of his cup and asked, "What has even done? The reason he was in here in the first place was because I was commending him on stopping a robbery!"

"It doesn't matter, Sheriff. Do you know where he lives? I gotta find this bastard."

The Sheriff was silent for a moment before shaking his head. "No, actually. Never had the pleasure of knowing."

"Dammit." The Marshall cursed, putting his hands on his hips and looking down.

"But I'm sure there's plenty of folk out there who do. Just ask around, you'll find him." The Sheriff suggested. The Marshall looked back up at the Sheriff. "Just… hide that badge. I don't know what it is, but people around here trust a badge about as much as they would trust a snake. Must be the reputation of the old sheriff."

The Marshall shook his head and stormed out of the building after saying, "Fine then". He approached his horse, grabbed his rolled up blue duster off of her and threw it on over his shiny badge. The lawman patted his horse. "It's gonna be a long day, girl." He scouted the town square for stagnate people to inquire with and his eyes fell upon an elderly lady sitting on a bench outside of a drug store. He applied one more pat to his horse before approaching the woman. She seemed to be reading a book, and her attention was deep within it. The Marshall felt bad when he had to interrupt her study.

"Excuse me ma'am," He said. The woman looked up from her book and placed her finger where she had stopped reading. "Sorry to interrupt, but I just need to ask you a quick question."

"Well, go on and ask, I haven't got all day!" She barked.

"Uh, do you happen to know a fella named John Falcon? And where he might live?" The Marshall asked somewhat timidly. The old woman recoiled in shock very calmly, as you might expect an old woman to do. "Oh," She begins. "I do know that name actually… I don't know where he lives, but he was the feller that shot that bastard in the general store a few days ago. I was there ordering my cans of vegetables, you see." The old woman explains. The Marshall nods, somewhat annoyed at the lack of progress he made by chatting with this woman.

"Thanks anyway." He says before walking off. The old woman returns to her book. The Marshall jumped from person to person, asking if they knew where he could find this misanthropic outlaw. He could conclude that John Falcon was a very quiet or secluded person, as little to no people knew who he was, and if they did, it was thanks to what he did at the general store that one evening. The lawman had no luck until he ended up at the north end of town, near a cattle corral.

The Marshall rubbed his nose and looked over to the corral, where a lone man sat, seemingly carving at a stick. The Marshall shook his head thinking what it could possibly hurt to ask this man if he knew the outlaw, despite all of his poor luck thus far. He approached this apparent cattleman. "Howdy friend!" He greeted. The man looked up and sheathed his knife and threw the stick. "Howdy," He replied.

The Marshall tipped his hat and put his hands to his hips, accidentally revealing his iron to the cattleman, who glanced at it and suddenly changed his demeanor. "Er, uh… How can I help?" He said. The Marshall was confused by this sudden change, but went with it anyway.

"Do you happen to know a feller named John Falco-"

"John Falcon? Yeah, I know John. He ain't here... b-but he lives just over there!" The man interrupted, speaking very quickly, very anxiously. He pointed to a small abode just down the road. In his mind, the Marshall was elated that he had finally found someone that knew this bastard. It was then when he looked down and noticed his six-shooter was exposed. The lawman then understood why the cattleman was so anxious, as he misinterpreted his hip-holding as intimidation. Of course, the Marshall didn't mean to intimidate the cattleman, but he succeeded in finding the outlaw's home that way.

"Thanks, my friend." He said, patting the man on the shoulder before walking towards the outlaw's home. "Y-you're welcome."

The Marshall looked forward to turning this John Falcon in so that he could finally get home to his family. As he stepped up onto the porch of this old log house, he couldn't help but grin. The lawman knocked on the door and placed his hand over his revolver, over his duster in anticipation of the outlaw opening the door. He waited and his hands sweat, watching as the door knob turned over and the door slowly opened, and on the other end… a short, blue-eyed woman. Shocked, the Marshall moved his hand onto his hip.

"Uh, hello there sir," The woman said in a shy voice. "Can I help you with something?"

"Er, yeah actually." The Marshall tipped his hat to the woman, his guard as down as a lame horse, as she scanned him up and down.

"Let's talk out here, please, have a seat." She directed as she closed the door behind her and sat on a rocking chair. The incognito lawman sat down on a dining chair there beside her. "I'm looking for a man, I was told he lived here. John Falcon. You know him?" He explained.

She looked at him once more and asked, "You a lawman?". Sensing suspicion in her voice, the Marshall decided to lie. "No ma'am, I'm an old acquaintance of his. I've been looking to reconnect, you see."

"Ah…" She nodded. "You must be Little Joe… You *are* small. John told me about you." The woman said. "Nice to know he's still talking about me." The Marshall furthered the lie despite taking a bit of offense to the name.

"Yeah, he does. I reckon you'll think he's changed. Damn fool ran off with one of those Glaser brothers over there. I saw it through my window." She described, pointing to the cattleman and his corral. It finally dawned on the Marshall that the cattleman meant that John was literally not in town at the moment. He felt somewhat defeated but he kept that to himself.

"Do you think he'll come back?" 'Little Joe' asked.

The woman began to stand up. "He better if he doesn't want to sleep on the dinner table tonight." She said before continuing. "Look, I don't mean any offense, mister, but I'm not quite in the mood for company… I had a sour morning. I'll come find you when he gets back, alright?"

This worked for the Marshall, who replied with "Sure, I'd appreciate that. Thank you."

The woman nodded and went back inside before the Marshall stood up and walked off the porch. As he began his walk back to his steed that was still hitched at the Sheriff's Office, he thought about his next move. He knew obviously that this lady had to be John Falcon's wife, but he didn't dwell on that thought. He knew he had to take John Falcon regardless. The lawman figured the next best thing to do would be to make his identity known to the rest of the town so as to avoid chaos in the event that the Marshall would have to shoot the outlaw. He changed his destination from his horse to the gallows in the center of town.

The Marshall knew that John would come home eventually, so he just had to wait him out. He had the trap set. The outlaw's own wife would lead the Marshall right to his target. He walked up the steps to the hanging stage and rang the bell that hung there to get the attention of everyone in the somewhat still-crowded square. They turned to the stage after finishing whatever they may have been doing and a crowd slowly gathered. The Marshall looked into it, seeing some of who he had talked to into the crowd, including the cattleman. The Sheriff walked out onto his patio to see the commotion.

"Excuse me y'all," The Marshall began as he reached into his blue duster, which from all of the walking he had done, had become dusty. "I know I'm a stranger to these parts, but I have an announcement to make." And the Sheriff stepped down off of his patio and into the crowd. The Marshall continued.

"Because you see, it's because I'm a stranger that I make this announcement." He unclipped his badge from his vest and clipped it back onto the duster. "I'm a Territorial Marshall of Arizona. Now, I won't be too long here in town. I'm here to take an outlaw by the name of John Falcon. Some of you may know this man." The Marshall quickly wiped the sweat from his head with his hat before continuing.

"But I'm certain that many of you didn't *know* that this man was an outlaw. Truth is… Truth is, John Falcon is vicious, a killer of his fellow man. A robber, a thief, all kinds of undesirable. Which is why… It is *very* important that no one interferes when I go to take this sorry excuse for a man in."

The crowd stared at the lawman, and he knew what they were thinking. He knew they felt lied to, that this stranger came in asking about this outlaw and lied straight to their faces, but it was all thanks to the Sheriff's advice. And just then, that very soul wandered up onto the stage as well. He spoke loudly and very clearly.

"If anyone interferes in the business of this here Territorial Marshall, well… you'll have to answer to me."

The Marshall nodded. "The outlaw isn't here right now, but if anyone sees him ride on in, you let me know, QUIETLY." He said. The crowd was silent, seemingly dumbfounded. "That's it! Now go on, git! Go back to your business!" The Sheriff barked.

The crowd dispersed and the Marshall turned to the Sheriff. "Thank you."

"Yeah, well… I just feel betrayed by this bastard. I hope you get him… He's pretty fast, from what I heard about what happened at the general store." The Sheriff said before returning to his office.

The Marshall would be lying if he said that the Sheriff's rumor hadn't worried him a bit. The Marshall was fast with his iron, but he wasn't sure if he would be faster than this fabled outlaw. He had to remind himself that there was nothing special about John Falcon. He's just lucky. He returned to his horse hitched up and gave her a pat and a carrot from the saddlebag. "We're on our way home soon girl." He muttered to her before sitting down next to her.

After a moment, the Marshall is woken up by a man with a familiar voice speaking to him. "E-excuse me, sir."

Startled by the voice, he pushed his hat up and looked around. He's still in Punto Muerto, but he's just realized that he fell asleep. The lawman looked up at the voice's origin, revealing it to be the cattleman.

"Sorry sir, didn't mean to startle you." He said. The Marshall stood up, though very slowly as he felt his age catch up to him thanks to his sleeping on the raw ground. "It's no problem," The Marshall assured. "What is it?"

"It's just uh…" The cattleman began trembling a bit. "The outlaw… uh, John Falcon's back!" The cattleman said, and suddenly, the lawman was fully awake. His eyes widened with shock. "Thank you for telling me, partner." The Marshall said as he patted his horse and unhitched her.

"Uh, of course, Marshall sir…" The cattleman stood where he was, watching as the Marshall lit up a smoke and mounted his steed before trotting to the home of the outlaw.

Around the bend towards the outside of town, the lawman looked towards the home of the woman and John Falcon. He saw them sitting on the porch together, seemingly chatting. He walked his horse to the corral where he hopped off and discarded his cigarette before tying her up to the fence. The last bit of smoke from the cigarette was wonderful, and a reminder of his children who complained about it and that he'd see them soon. The anticipation of catching this outlaw made time go slow for the

Marshall. He heard nothing but his footsteps as he slowly approached the log home, trying not to sway his right hand too much to keep it near the gun. As he neared, he saw the couple break out of an embrace and the woman, who as he recalled, was absent from his speech at the gallows, looked at him.

The Territorial Marshall was close enough now that he was ready to act on his mentally jotted plan. He heard the woman speak, but not what she said. The Marshall called out as he watched the blonde-haired young man, who was likely the outlaw he had been searching for, glance at him.

"John Falcon!" And the man squinted at the Marshall and slowly stood up before very carefully walking down the steps. "That's me. What do you want?" John Falcon asked, still focusing on the Marshall. The adrenaline began to assault the lawman's body.

In an attempt to subside it, he rubbed his mustache and smacked at the tail of his duster coat, throwing it back. As it fell back down, it got caught behind the holster that held his six-shooter.

"You rob a bank in El Paso?" He asked, focusing too hard on the movements of the outlaw to notice the crowd gathering at a distance behind him. He watched the expressions of the misanthrope, seeing a rage build up inside of him, and he offhandedly noticed that the outlaw wore his holster on the front of his belt instead of the side, like everyone else. The outlaw spit before speaking again.

"Unlikely… why?" He lied. The Marshall laughed out loud after a failed attempt to contain it, as he found this response so idiotic. He had been studying this outlaw for the past day and knew what he knew. The lawman decided to go for a more violent crime to build up that rage that was brewing in John Falcon.

"Maybe you killed a rancher and his wife because he wouldn't give you his safe-"

"WHO ARE YOU?!" The outlaw rudely interrupted. The Marshall knew his rage had peaked and he himself had grown more confident. He adjusted his hat with his left hand to keep his right hand free for the gun and introduced himself.

"I'm a Territorial Marshall. I'm here to take you in, John Falcon."

"Like hell you are!" The outlaw yelled. "Ain't you a bit out of your jurisdiction anyway?"

The Marshall thought to himself for a moment. This outlaw clearly wasn't very bright. Punto Muerto is in his jurisdiction, because it's in Arizona. He thought of something witty to say and came up with, "I was in town, figured I'd stop in."

Just then, the Marshall watched as the woman finally stood up and rushed to the railing of their home's porch. "John!" She yelled to her outlaw husband. "It's alright Flo." John said in an attempt to console her, but the Marshall could see that she was still nervous. He didn't want to worry the woman, he just wanted to do his job and bring this outlaw in. He would prefer to bring him in alive, but he knew he had to make it known to John that he would kill if need be.

"Look, I didn't come all this way to put a bullet in your thick skull. I don't want to kill you, but trust me… If you make me, I will." He stated.

"Right," The outlaw said in response. This sparked a bit of hope in the Marshall that maybe, just maybe John Falcon would simply surrender here, but alas, he continued, and that spark was snuffed as instantly as it was made. "Guess you're just gonna have to kill me then…" and the outlaw reached for his six-shooter. The Marshall was ready to draw his weapon and jump behind some cover, as he was always a better shot at a distance.

"Wait!" Suddenly, the woman ran down the steps and jumped in the middle of the two men, and John moved his hand away from his weapon. The Marshall did not, however.

"W-why don't you duel? That's fair, ain't it?" She suggested. This threw a pit in the Marshall's stomach. The very word 'duel' frightened him. It was how his beloved brother died. A gunshot from an outlaw in a duel. And just then he was reminded of his dream from last night, how his rotting brother said that the Marshall would be there to watch him hang in hell. Unfortunately, he let his sudden fear get the best of him, and he began to tremble so very subtly.

"I reckon I'll let you decide, Marshall." The Outlaw said, making a display of his arrogance.

And stupidly, oh so stupidly, the Marshall blurted, "Fine," He instantly realized his mistake but also knew that to retract his decision would be foolish. He visibly shook further. All he could do now was insist on the rules. "Forty feet, John. Got it? Let's go to the street."

"Sure, forty feet. And just for you, I'll move my leather down to my side… to give you a fightin' chance." The Outlaw agreed arrogantly. The two began to move to the greater street in the area, and the Marshall watched as a crowd gathered further. In his head, the Marshall was very nervous, frightened even. He was doomed. He knew it to be true. He had a shot of killing this outlaw, but the thought of his dream had startled him, and now he shook violently.

At a range of forty feet, the lawman counted his breaths as he held his shaking hand close to his pistol after moving the duster away again. The crowd that had been chattering had fallen silent. He watched as John Falcon moved his goofy holster to his hip. Suddenly, the outlaw spoke up.

"That's a mighty big iron you got there, Marshall. Will you even be able to lift it quick enough?"

The Marshall breathed out and retorted, "You just worry about yourself, scum." and as he spoke, the shakiness of his body had spread to his words as well.

"Don't be scared, Marshall. It'll all be over soon. All of this." The Outlaw taunted.

The Marshall ignored that line and breathed in and held it, trying to focus, but no matter how hard he tried to silence his mind, he heard everything. He could focus in on his adversary just fine, it was the noises that were distracting. The wind blew around debris from all over and he heard a mumble in the crowd, a mumble that had caught his attention and made everything so much worse.

"That handsome Territorial Marshall is a goner…"

BANG!

<u>John Falcon</u>

John Falcon sat at his old and worn dining table. He smoked a cigarette as he read the Punto Muerto Gazette. He scanned the lines of words as he puffed smoke from his mouth, which blew up into his blonde hair. John heard the creaking of his home's floorboards and looked up to see his wife walking into the Kitchen. She made a pitstop to kiss the rugged man on his forehead, which he met with a smile, before proceeding to the cast iron stove. It heated eggs and sizzled bacon that waited for the couple to dig into them.

"Good morning, hon." Flo said to him as he flicked his cigarette, ridding it of its ash. "Good mornin'."

John put the newspaper down and readied his metal plate before looking over to his wife. "Did the boy get to school?" He asked. Flo looked back at him.

"He did," She answered, waiting a moment to say something that lingered on her mind. "He told me about how excited he was to go fishing with you later today." John laughed a bit.

"Yeah, I told him yesterday that we'd go fishin' just in the river to the south." John explained. "It's been too long."

Flo nodded as she stirred the bacon around. "Yeah," She was silent for a moment. "He also told me about some boy that's been beating on him." John appeared somewhat concerned.

"Really?" He said bluntly in disbelief. Flo grabbed the pan of food and dished it out onto the plates. She sat down. "Yeah, says he badgers him for his food like… like a damn badger!"

John tapped at his bacon for a moment before looking back up at his wife, into her deep blue eyes.

"Well, then the boy needs to stand up for himself. Knock this kid into next week." John dictated. Flo looked back at her husband after taking a bite of egg.

"Maybe… Maybe he should just tell a teacher. He doesn't have to get violent." She suggested. John retorted.

"A teacher ain't gonna do anythin' about it. This brat's gotta be taught a lesson. He won't bother the boy again if he knows he can throw a punch." Flo looked back down at her food for a moment, sliding her fork under a bit of bacon. She looked back up at John.

"Do you really want him to be that way? How you… were?" She questioned the man.

"How I was? Flo, there's robbin' and killin' people and then there's just self defense." He explained, using his hands to categorize the two forms of violence. "You're right John, but where is the line?" The woman asked to counter the argument.

"What if he gets a taste for it? The power? I've slapped a man or two in my lifetime, I know it can feel good to have that... You would know, look at that damn pistol hanging up by the door with twenty notches."

The former outlaw snaps, "And you know damn well I ain't done that anymore!" He stands up and rushes towards the front door, floorboards creaking the whole way. "And they was all bastards anyway!" He finished as Flo attempted to follow him.

"You don't mean that. You *don't* mean that." She said, her voice shaky. John scoffed as he put on his belt where the aforementioned notched pistol had been holstered, which was on the front of his belt as opposed to the usual hip placement. He opened the door, stepping out. "I got places to be."

John walked away from his small home and shook his head. Something felt off about today. It was still early in the morning but he could sense that something was different. Maybe it was just his irritation, an emotion he never felt in the early morning. John Falcon was a morning person. Many long nights that stretched into dawn he spent on stakeouts back in the day. He had to be very attentive, so he was. He noticed every little detail. And he was very fast because of that.

John always liked the name that his reputation of attentiveness gave him. He thought falcons, or any raptor, was majestic. Claws for food, feathers for soaring… and a beak for pecking. Simple, yet so deadly. Nobody in the town of Punto Muerto knew why John was called Falcon, and that was okay. After all, the whole point of himself and his family moving into Arizona was to find anonymity.

Watching the armed guards, learning their patterns and figuring when the best time to "go in" would be. Who would be the easiest to shoot, who was slowest on the draw. All of this scoping out he spent a good portion of his still young life doing. He was just fourteen when he put the first notch on his pistol. Thinking about this made him smile, not because he had ended someone, but because he had met Flo that year. They were the same age, and some might've said it was love at first sight.

Their son was born a mere four years after they met, whence they reconciled after John had spent some time in Oklahoma. And in the present day still, John was but a youth of twenty-four. He was snapped out of his thoughts when he heard a voice with a deep southern accent call out to him. "John!"

John looked around and found himself by a corral, and on the fence of said corral was, to John, a great irritant, and thus, someone he avoided in the mornings. "Hey Leonard, it's John Falcon!" The voice called to someone else. John sighed before putting on his friendly face and approaching the two men.

"Howdy fellers." John greeted. "What are the Glaser brothers doin' in town? This early?"

John looked around the corral and saw three pretty horses tied up next to a trough. In the corral he noticed a beautiful spotted Hereford heifer.

"Pa wanted us to bring this ole heifer in to try to get her sold." Dan Glaser explained. The other brother, Leonard, got up on the fence too. "Say, you want her?"

"No, I ain't got no need for beef cattle at the moment," John said as he began to walk away. "But I'll let folk know there's a cow out here for sale." The two brothers smiled.

"Moo-cho Grassy-ass, partner!" Leonard thanked. "Mmhmm."

John continued into the greater area of Punto Muerto. What he said earlier was true, he did have places to be. He was expected at the Sheriff's office today and John had no idea what for. This in turn, made him somewhat anxious as he did realize this again. He was worried that the sheriff had possibly figured out what John had done in the past. He had only been to a sheriff's office once before in his life, and it was so long ago he couldn't remember what it was for. He had managed to evade the law during his long tenure as an outlaw.

John steadied himself as he approached the office. He walked by the gallows, trying to push intrusive thoughts of 'are they going to hang you?' out of his head. Arizona dust blew in the wind as it picked up. He quickly wandered up the steps and entered the white office building before the dust could blow too hard into his face, patting himself up before looking up and into the room. Sitting behind a desk is the sheriff, who wears a fine white hat. "Howdy, John." The sheriff greets. He sips on a glass of whiskey.

The office is dimly-lit, with only a few lanterns hanging up from the ceiling and walls, with none in the cells which were plainly visible to the public.

"Howdy… you called for me sir." John said, cringing a bit in his mind as he had never taken to calling anyone 'sir'. The sheriff nodded and opened his drawer. "I reckon I did."

John shook slightly but maintained his composure. The Sheriff spoke again.

"Interesting to see you put your holster for your iron on the front of your belt like that, never seen that before. You're obviously very fast with it that way."

John wasn't sure what the sheriff was reaching for. Was it a six-shooter? Was it a trap of some kind? John put his hand on his hips so if need be, he could get to his gun quickly. He watched attentively as the sheriff reached into the drawer, in case he needed to douse the rumor of his swiftness in truth. The sheriff looked at John.

"Here you go." The sheriff throws a small wad of cash at the blonde-haired man. He looked it over, apparently confused. "What's this for?"

"I want to commend you for taking care of that robber in the general store. You're pretty damn fast with that gun of yours, so I heard. Hey, you want a drink?" The sheriff answered as he held up a bottle of whiskey. "Huh," John uttered as he thought about the notch he added to his pistol for this kill.

His anxiety perished away and he pocketed the cash. John began to walk out, attempting to leave this perceived hostile environment. "No thank you, Sheriff. But I'm happy I could help, it was my pleasure."

He froze as realized what he said. The Sheriff perked up before taking another sip of his whiskey. "Your pleasure?" He questioned. John's anxiety had suddenly surfaced again. He couldn't muster up any sort of word that would make sense.

"Well I like a man like that," The sheriff said, allowing John to breathe again. He continued, "Maybe stop back by the office sometime... you interested in working as a lawman?" John turned back around.

"Uh… that doesn't sound too bad." John admitted. He thought it could be a good way to "reform" maybe. In any case, this is a good opportunity. "We got thieves and highwaymen from here to Santa Fe need clearing out. Could use the help." The Sheriff explained.

"I'll think on it. See what the wife thinks." John said, the sheriff chuckled. "Ah, I know how that is." The sheriff stood up and extended his hand. "I hope to see you back in here, John."

John shook the sheriff's hand, though rather weakly. He realized it was the first time he ever truly shook someone's hand.

As the former outlaw opened the door to leave, he accidentally bumped into another man walking in. And normally this would frustrate him, and he would resort immediately to provoking this man in some way, but instead he simply apologized. Something happened in the Sheriff's office, something happened when he shook the sheriff's hand. John felt as though a new chapter in his life could finally begin. A job as a lawman could help him truly start anew, as he had tried to do when he first moved his family to Punto Muerto.

And again, his thoughts fell on Flo. He felt guilty for snapping at her. John realized that he had simply taken out a pent up anger on her. He was excited to return home to her and apologize. With his cash reward from the Sheriff, he wanted to take her out to a nice dinner at the local saloon maybe. She would like that. He remembered why he loved her… She's strong, erudite. The perfect kind of person to have in life, or at least, his life. His thoughts were interrupted as a familiar yell was heard from nearby. John looked up and noticed he was back by the corral where the Glaser brothers were attempting to sell the heifer, having been lost in thought for the majority of the walkback.

The two brothers were yelling at each other in the corral and as John looked further, he noticed that the heifer was no longer there. He approached the corral and interrupted the two squabbling men.

"Hey fellers, where's your cow?" He queried. Leonard pushes his brother away and approaches the fence. "This mo-ron left the gate open and the heifer got out and jolted into the desert!"

"Well you said you was gonna shut the damn thing!" Dan retorted. "Oh hush, you mo-ron! We gotta go get her back now!" Leonard rushes to grab a line of lasso hung upon the fence.

"Please, can you help us since you're here, John?" Dan begged. John rubbed his light stubble, thinking. He still felt good. "Oh, what the hell. Let's get this heifer." John walks towards a group of hitched horses. Leonard grabs another bit of rope and throws it to John before directing him. "You can take Tess, she's the strawberry roan."

Dan begins to walk towards his own nag, but Leonard interjects. "Nuh-uh, you've done enough, stay here!" Dan throws his hands up. "Oh, you don't want my help? Fine, you idiot!" And he returned to the corral, leaning up against a wood post of the barbed wooden fence with his arms crossed.

The two men saddle up and ride into the desert, kicking up the dust beneath the hooves as they gallop. "She couldn't have gone far," John hypothesized. "She's old. Can't run very fast."

Leonard scoffed, "Pa told me a story one time, he was wrangling cattle out of Kansas and there was a heifer ran faster than a wild stallion!"

"Well it's a good thing we ain't chasin' that heifer." John barked.

They furthered into the desert, John keeping his eyes peeled despite the flying sand from the hooves of their steeds. He scanned the arid landscape like a bird searching for a meal. His skills he once used to rob and steal, he used in the assistance of another for the first time in his life.

They rode for, to him, a very long half hour before they found the heifer by a small pond surrounded by old dry trees. The brother spent the whole time jaw-jacking and it was chipping away at John's pleasant mood, but it persisted. It made him realize that what he was doing was very uncharacteristic for him. He never liked to work with others, even during his outlaw days. Flo always called him a lone wolf, to his chagrin.

Eventually, the duo waited on a small hill looking down upon the lost animal. Leonard spit before leaning over on his pommel. "Alright, so here's what we'll do…" John interrupted him.

"Let's just run down there and grab the damn heifer. Leonard, you guide her to me and I'll rope her up."

The brother sat on his steed silently, just looking at the man. "Jesus, let's go." John waved the boy to follow him, and he did. Maybe he was shocked at the sudden turn of emotion, or maybe he was just scared. They acted on the plan nonetheless. As the nags galloped down the hill, dust was thrown into the air. Leonard rushed toward the beast, startling it. He got to the side to push the animal in the direction of the former outlaw, who had steadied himself just nearby.

The orange, kicked-up dust had formed into somewhat of a localized storm. The cow that had been shook didn't help it any, as its hooves threw more of the dust into the air. It rushed towards John, who readied his lasso. It mooed as it ran faster, to John's surprise. He had little to no experience with cattle, save for the occasional wrangling gigs he picked up in his younger youth.

"It's comin' at ya John!" Leonard called from behind the veil of dust. In response, John quickly threw the lasso blindly into the dust, and after a moment he felt a tug on the rope. He quickly tied it to the pommel of the saddle. The tugging visibly became more violent as the rope tightened on the saddle, and smoke rose from the pommel thanks to the friction. The air was silent, and despite the Glaser brother's presence, not a word was spoken.

As the dust began to settle, what had happened had become apparent. The lost heifer was adorned with the lasso of the former outlaw. The duo of wranglers erupted into a cheer, even John.

"Yeehaw!"

"Good throw John!"

They spent a moment celebrating their victory before beginning their journey home, another half hour trip.

When they returned, it was maybe ten past eleven in the morning. John still had a little grin on his face as they put the cow back in the corral. "Thanks again, John!" Leonard said. Dan, who helped guide the animal back into the corral, appeared somewhat shaken. "Say, good work John… uh, I should… I need to tell you something…" He said shakily.

"What's wrong?" John questioned.

"Well, er… there was a fella that came to me… he was looking for you. I told him you were gone but… Well, I told him where you live. He's a… well… I don't know." Dan explained.

John was confused but couldn't help but mentally shrug. "Thanks for telling me, pard. I'll ask Flo about him." He said. Leonard piped up as he left the corral. "Hey, thanks again partner!"

"You're welcome fellers, just uh… try to keep that gate closed, yeah?" John teased, his pleasant mood showing no signs of slowing down.

"I'll remember to remind this fool." Leonard said, slapping Dan on the back. "Oh hell, I'll remind you!" Dan snarled.

John walked off after hitching the horse with the strawberry roan coat. He looked around in the vicinity and saw some townsfolk looking at him, but he couldn't see their expressions thanks to dirt that had accumulated in his eye. He rubbed his eyes and looked to his home and noticed that on the porch sat his wife, Flo. Remembering his thoughts from earlier, John rushed to the house. He again looked around and saw the townsfolk that gave him strangely worried expressions. As he got closer to home, he noticed Flo's face of disappointment. He slowed down and took a step onto the porch step before looking up at his wife who sat on a rocking chair.

"Where'd you run off to with that boy?" Flo asked him coldly. "You rustle some cattle?"

John sighed, "No dear," He walked up onto the porch finally and sat next to her on a standard chair. Being closer to her, he heard the creaks as she rocked the chair back and forth. He continued, "No, I went on and helped them get their heifer back. Their pa wants it sold." Flo didn't say anything for a moment.

"That's not like you." She stated. John nodded and put his hands on his knees, leaning forward.. "I know. I'm in a good mood."

Flo looked over at her husband, her face spelling both confusion and irritation.

"I got offered a job by the Sheriff," He explained. "I would be a lawman. Clear the roads of… bad folk." John looks down at his feet.

"So that's what that was about?" Flo understood. "Yeah… I- Flo, I understand if you don't want me to do this, It's just…" John stuttered as he struggled to find words, probably for the first time in his life.

"It's just what?" Flo pressed, as she looked back out into town, her red hair blowing in the slight breeze. John proceeded to explain.

"It's just that, when I moved us out here I thought it would be a new chapter for us, like in a story book, you know? We would get away from everythin' that happened before and… we could start somethin' new, give our boy a fightin' chance in this world. But just because we moved here… well, nothin's changed." Flo looked back at her husband.

"John, you speak like you regret what you did all those years." She said, and John was silent for a moment. "I was wrong this morning, Flo." He wiped his hands on his pants.

"I was wrong. None of them who I killed deserved it. Not one night passes… that I don't remember their faces or their screams when I… In truth, I do… I do regret it. Every night, I pay that price."

Flo's face shifted from irritated to disheartened. "Why didn't you ever tell me?" She asked the man. "I didn't want to worry you. You already have a lot to worry about."

Flo shifted her chair a bit to face her husband a bit better.

"Anyway… I just thought that by becomin' a lawman, things could finally start gettin' better. We can finally have the life we dreamed of when we was watchin' the stars out in Texas." John reminisced.

His wife couldn't help but smile. She leaned in to hug him and they met halfway between the two pieces of furniture for an embrace. She whispered in his ear. "I think you should do whatever you think is best, hon." He nodded as he laid his head on her shoulder. "I will then."

However, John's attentiveness kicked in again. In the corner of his eye, he saw a large, shadowy figure moving towards his home. He quickly released his wife from the embrace, which took her by surprise a bit. She appeared that way until she looked out into the town and saw the figure approaching as well. Flo returned her attention to her husband, who still looked at the figure, and told him, "Oh, look who decided to come see you again! Little Joe!"

"John Falcon!" The figure called out, unknowingly interrupting. John was focused on the figure, his face expressing this as he slowly stood up. This was not his old friend from childhood, Little Joe. He walked down the steps of the porch, his wife watching with great confusion. "That's me." He responded to the figure. "What do you want?"

The figure rubbed his mustache before throwing his blue duster coat back, revealing a six-shooter. He spoke and said, "You rob a bank in El Paso?" John looked around as he noticed an ample amount of townsfolk gathering nearby.

"Unlikely," John responded. "Why?" To this, the stranger chuckled, and he spoke again.

"Maybe you killed a rancher and his wife because he wouldn't give you his safe-"

"Who are you?!" John yelled, growing nervous as the stranger correctly called out his old crimes. The stranger flicked his hat straight and said, "I'm a Territorial Marshall. I'm here to take you in, John Falcon."

"Like hell you are! Ain't you a bit out of your jurisdiction anyway?" John warned as he scanned the stranger up and down, seeing a shiny badge. "I was in town, figured I'd stop in." The Marshall retorted. Flo stood up from her chair and leaned against the porch railing. "John!" She called. "It's alright Flo." He comforted her.

"Look," The Marshall began. "I didn't come all this way to put a bullet in your thick skull. I don't want to kill you, but trust me… If you make me, I will."

John nodded demeaningly. "Right," he scoffed. "Guess you're just gonna have to kill me then…" John reached for his pistol, and the Marshall followed suit. Flo ran down off the porch and separated the men. "WAIT!" and they froze and looked at her.

"W-why don't you duel? That's fair, ain't it?" She suggested with every confidence that her husband was the faster gunman. Confident as well, John returned his sight to the Marshall and nodded. "I reckon I'll let you decide, Marshall."

The Marshall squinted and moved his hand away from his large weapon. "Fine," he said, moving away ever so slightly. He appeared somewhat shaken now, and this planted a seed of confidence in John.

"Forty feet, John. Got it? Let's go to the street." The duelists began to make their way to the road by the family's house. John spoke up.

"Sure, forty feet. And just for you, I'll move my leather down to my side… to give you a fightin' chance."

John watched while he adjusted his holster as townsfolk gathered nearby, even seeing as people peered out their windows. The Glaser brothers looked on, and even the sheriff appeared. The Marshall moved his coat out of the way, revealing his six-shooter again. John observed it closely, seeing its long barrel. "That's a mighty big iron you got there, Marshall." He said.

"Will you even be able to lift it quick enough?"

"You just worry about yourself, scum." The Marshall growled, his voice shaking to John's notice, and he took advantage of this. The Marshall was scared.

"Don't be scared, Marshall. It'll all be over soon. All of this."

They were distanced forty feet from each other and John put his hand close to his Iron, following suit with the Marshall. The town fell deathly silent. To John, it seemed as though the spectators were holding their breath with anticipation. He knew they knew what was going to happen. His reputation as a fast gunman had spread like a virus after what happened at the general store that one evening, after John's 'twentieth notch'. He quickly glanced around, and his eyes fell on his beautiful wife, who spectated by the house.

She appeared just as nervous as everyone else in the crowds, and for some reason, that made John feel better. He smiled at her and thought about how excited he was to take her to dinner after this was all over. He thought about taking his son to the river to fish. He thought about what he would really teach his son when it came to dealing with bullies. But first, John had to deal with his own bully. His eyes returned to the Marshall and he stared him down.

John breathed steadily and watched the Marshall, and even at forty feet he noticed that he was shaky, his hand trembling by his pistol. The only noise to grace his ears was that of the wind blowing pebbles around, but his focus brought him back to the moment and that sound was drowned out when suddenly…

BANG!

<u>Epilogue</u>

John Falcon had not cleared leather, for a bullet fairly ripped from the revolver of the Territorial Marshall. John's gun, while barely grasped by his hand, fell back into its holster. The resounding bang of the Marshall's gun had finally silenced when the body of the outlaw fell back onto the dirt. The crowd remained silent only after their collective gasp. The Marshall breathed out finally, gasping for air as he threw his hands on his knees and bent over before holstering the smoking gun.

"NOOOOOOOO!" A scream from the crowd erupted. Flo ran out to her dead husband. "NO NO NO, GOD DAMMIT!" She cried out as she touched his bleeding face. The Marshall stood up straight as he had finally caught some air, and he approached the body and Flo. She cradled John's head as she cried and pushed back his blood-soaked blonde hair, looking into his still open hazel eyes. The Marshall stood three feet back from them and he watched her cry as his shaking finally stopped.

"I'm sorry…" Were the words he managed to say as he took his hat off and held it down by his stomach. Flo continued to cry but looked up at the Marshall.

"You bastard… you bastard…" She lamented. The Marshall didn't say anything.

She cried further. "He was a changed man, you bastard! He was… he was gonna be a lawman… he was gonna take his boy fishing today!"

The Marshall stood there but shifted his eyes to the ground. He couldn't stop the liquid shame from filling his body where the adrenaline of apprehension once stilled, and yet, he still didn't say anything. Flo looked down at her deceased spouse, closed his eyes, and spoke one last time to the Marshall before bellowing out the harvest of her newfound melancholy.

"What am I gonna tell the boy…" And the Marshall waited a moment before putting his hat back on. He turned around and looked at the crowd which still stood.

"I…" He began, but failed to finish.

The lawman wasted no more time before slowly moving to his horse and unhitching her. He figured the best he could do for the woman he widowed was to not loot John Falcon's body for the bounty, the proof of kill. Thus, he would go unpaid for this one. He mounted his steed and slowly walked through the crowd and beyond them, the sound of the crying woman slowly fading away in the distance. The Territorial Marshall felt no emotion. To him, it was just another job. He just walked and patted his horse as they went through the now-empty town square, and distant from the spot of the duel.

But suddenly, he heard a screech from high above him. He looked up and took his hat off to have a better field of view, and it took him a moment to see what may have made that noise as the sun glared in his eyes. When it blocked it out for a moment, he saw a falcon gliding so majestically in the wind. It's brown wings straight, just floating, waiting for the slightest glance of something to eat. Maybe it would find what it was looking for, or maybe it already did…

Maybe this falcon just wanted to fly. Fly, not because it was hunting to survive, but because it had never felt that true feeling of flying freedom. The freedom of never having to watch for predators, never having to worry about its kin in its nest, or never having to give all of its strength just to stay afloat. The freedom to soar to the highest heights it could possibly go.